Unapologetically Imperfect

KC Hampton

Presentation by *BookLeaf Publishing*

Web: www.bookleafpub.com

E-mail: info@bookleafpub.com

ISBN : 9789394788824

First edition 2022

DEDICATION

This incredible story is dedicated to my loved ones watching over me, especially my Gramma, that has guided me through this challenging thing called life. Without heartbreak and grief, I would have never found my way to the words that set me free. So here's to you; thank you for giving me my wings.

ACKNOWLEDGEMENT

I want to thank my editor, confidant, friend, supporter, the first reader of my work, and most importantly, my Aunt, Amanda Giliberti. Without you, it would all be rubbish scattered on the page.

I also want to give thanks to my Mom and Dad. However, the two words "Thank you" do not fill the amount of gratitude I feel for them. There are not enough words in the dictionary to describe the love and support they give me every day to make this dream come true. I take the life they have provided me for granted and try to remind myself how truly blessed I am. Thank you for being my friends, supporters, the loudest person at any stage, being my strength when I am weak, and my words when I cannot speak.

Family is everything to me, and I thank them all for being by my side. Especially my adorable fur baby, Buca, who always knows how to help me out of my writer's block, with lots of kisses.

Table of Contents

Lost For Words

I try to write down the words haunting my brain,
that get lost as they travel down to my hand,
but the only motion it's making, is shaking to
find the words.

My brain tries to communicate with my mouth,
but the waves get lost,
stuck somewhere between my mind and clogged
throat.

My Mom stares at me with her worried eyes,
begging me,
"Just one word. Just tell me what you need,
baby, please?"

I try to tell her, tugging her shirt pointing at the
thing that I am craving,
but my words are lost, as she's left to read my
mind like all Moms do best.

Year four flew by no matter how tight my
parents held on.

I was twelve before they knew it,

battling bullies even though I didn't attend
public school,
still managing to get ridiculed.

Seventeen came before I could even blink,
with lips that still have never been kissed
and gaining an unwelcoming hundred pounds to
my hips.

Crying looking at myself in the mirror still
trying to communicate with peers,
but didn't have anyone to call a friend, unsure
how to get them to stay until the end.

All in the same year finding out I have
Asperger's,
discovering the reason why I have a twisted
tongue and a delayed brain.

Not knowing much about Asperger's at the time,
I soon realized how much of a pain in the "asp"
it is.

I didn't let that stop me, instead in a way, it
made me stronger,
it made me want to prove it wrong,
that I could be more than a label the doctors
gave me.

Graduating with my loved ones' help
and my delayed brain trying to pull me down.

I went to college and started to change my life
around at nineteen,
started to lose weight and be the person I knew I
could be.

But before I could flip the page,
before I could continue on this journey,
a life-shattering event changed me, as my best
friend
and supporter through all this, gets ill,
as I hold her hand to the end and must say
farewell.

My Gramma was the light that told me I could
do anything
no matter what "title" I was given.

For a year I felt lost and broken,
like a scattered piece of window
that has just been bashed in by a foreign object,
making something that was once so polished
and shined with its innocence to this world,
now broken apart into tiny pieces with reality
shattering it from its rims,
not sure how to fight the words trying to find
their way

out of my mind and into the world before me.

Still dealing with bullies,
but this time I realized the biggest bully,
was myself,
looking in the mirror and not even seeing the
real me.

I got tired of feeling sorry for myself
and not giving myself the credit, I deserved.

The light inside of me changed
then year twenty I looked myself in the mirror
and finally said, "I love you."

My heart grew, with self-gratitude,
like rain falling down from the sky,
knowing it will turn into a rainbow,
as I decided to be proud of who I am
and stop pointing out my flaws
turning them into what makes me beautiful.

Year twenty-one, finally been kissed, had my
heart broken,
which added to its scars, and for the first time, I
found my words.

I took my hurt, from the past and present
turning them into something beautiful,

something wonderful, and understandable.

I wrote the thoughts in my head and kept
writing,
until the caulis on my fingers bled.

I wrote and found my soul.

Now twenty-two and I can't go a day without
putting my thoughts on paper,
but mainly on my phone,
with thoughts that grab and take me in the
middle of the night,
expressing how I feel into words and emotions,
which used to be so hard to find, but now is a
part of my life.

It's me written so neatly and finely.

This is my life, as a poem, it's me, written to a T,
tangled up with the truth and rawness of life.

I still have pain and demons that knock at my
door,
like we all do, but now I know how to handle
them.

With paper, a pen, and a heart that bleeds the
words calling out to me.

Hold my hand

I'll hold your hand for hours without even a
care,
I'm right here beside you just let me hold you
here,
and tell you I'm with you,
through it all until the end nears.

Let me tell you everything is okay,
everything will be fine,
I'll hold your hand forever,
just stay right here.

The inevitable beeping occurs,
you must leave me now
and I have to let go of your hand.

My heart gains a hole,
as I let go,
setting you free.

I leave you,
I walk away.

Closing my leaking eyes,
I reach out my hand
waiting for your fingers to grace mine.

A brisk of wind entangles my fingers,
then I hear a whisper,
"I'm right here, my dear. You held my hand until
the very end.
Now it's my turn, to guide you and never leave
you again."

You're still right here with me,
telling me you're okay.

You'll hold my hand through the sad times,
through the good and the bad.

You'll hold my hand down the aisle, someday.

You'll see me grow older,
and stronger every day.

Time keeps on moving with no pause or rewind.

As moments turn into memories without you in
them,
I wish you were here beside me,
but then I reach out my hand
and remember you are.

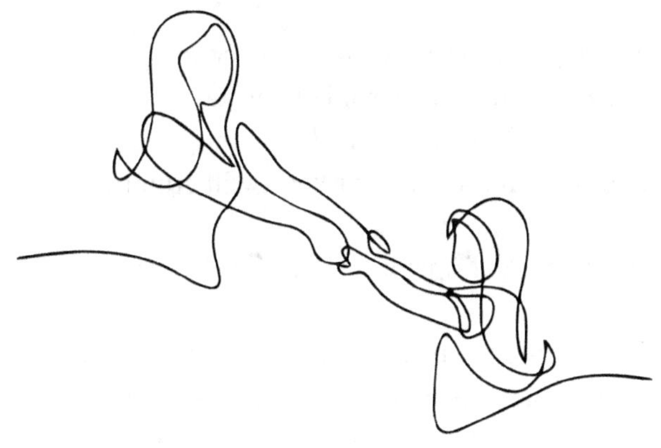

Missing Piece

Love is painful regardless
whether it's good or bad.

When you fall in love with someone,
it creates an indescribable pain,
like something grew inside of you
and if it's removed your heart will crumble.

It's a game of operation that can never be won.

Every time the tweezers get close to clean up the
broken pieces shattered within your soul,
the buzzer sets off causing a mild heart attack.

But the more you fall in love with a person
you realize something didn't just grow there,
something was missing and for the first time
you know what it feels like for your heart to beat
whole.

It's a thudding that rings in your ears
a sweet melody you've never heard before,

that sings through your veins all the way down
to your toes.

But if that piece is ever removed or altered
your heart will crumble to pit of your stomach
taking forever to rebuild again,
as you wonder if that missing piece will return
once more.

You never missed that feeling before,
because you never knew what it felt like,
but now that it's entered your life
you never want that feeling to go away.

Love is a mix concoction of emotions,
with a dash of promises,
a splash of child-like hope,
and a heavy hand of blinding trust.

Love is a game played by two,
that comes in many forms that disguises itself
in the glazed eyes of someone fallen head over
heels.

It's a game that should be played wisely
with a careful heart and a tamed mind,
as you prepare yourself to get addicted to
something so delicate it could break,
at any moment of time,

just by the blink of your eye.

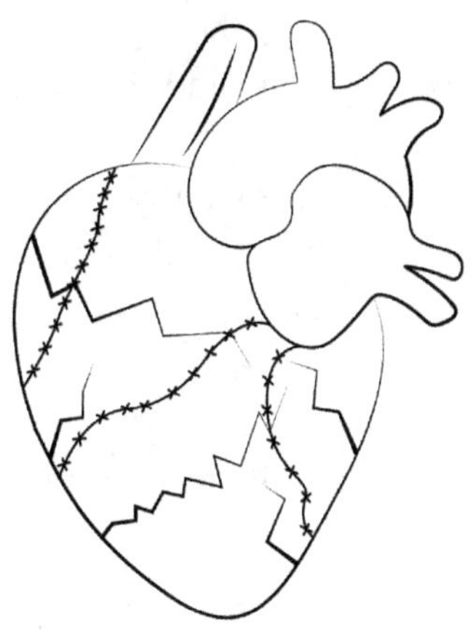

Surroundings

Water drizzles down my back,
as I let it wash away the day,
to take away the pain and sorrows.

Each drop finds its own rhythm,
as it taps my skin and drips to the floor,
creating a new beat.

Soap fragments the air tickling my nose
with the freshness of cucumber and lime.

Bitter green apple suds, escape from my hair,
leaking into the corners of my mouth.

A puddle forms in my shaky hands
as I cup them together to rinse my face.

I take in every feeling and motion,
the soft circles of my bath sponge lightly
scrubbing my pale skin
and the water tapping in the crook of my neck,
having this magic ability to take me away to a
place that doesn't exist.

Singing along with my obnoxiously loud music
pressing my vocal cords and eardrums to their
limits.

After spending hours,
what felt like days in a foreign room,
holding on to sorrow and pain.

As the beeping of monitors went silent.

Aroma of saline caught in the back of my throat
along with the bile that played peek-a-boo on
my taste buds.

As the person I love's hand fell from mine.

I do not cry,
I do not shed a tear
I am numb,
stuck in a dream.

Staying in the shower as long as I can
to let go of a day that has left me paralyzed
from head to toe.

The Prayer

Are you here with me,
do you even exist?

Am I allowed to ask that or just bow my head
and trust you'll wake me when dawn breaks
through the next day?

The darkness rushes over me,
they say it's all make believe,
I shouldn't feel the things inside of me,
if I truly believe.

The thing is, I don't know what is real
and what is just fantasy,
because when I close my eyes
and say a prayer sometimes it's just out of habit,
and sometimes out of fear.

Fear if I don't say anything to you,
I will leave this world and just disappear.

I will fall into an oblivion,
letting the darkness not only in
but let it win for eternity

and my soul will never be free of this burden.

They say you are love and nothing else,
but I've never known what that feels like,
so why do I bow my head
and speak to someone that might not be real.

Hope,
maybe that's all I need.

To hope that when I close my eyes
and give into the darkness
you'll be there to catch me.

Even though they say,
I will fall into the black hole of Hell
never to return again,
and my heart and soul will disappear.

I know that when I lay my head down to sleep,
you will take my soul,
no matter how much it has rotted,
even if I half believe.

Because why would I speak to open air,
if no one was listening or didn't care?

I take my last breath
and feel my worries disappear.

Falling, but for the first time with no fear.

My soul reincarnates,
for the first time knowing how to be loved,
for the first time knowing how to be awake.

And when I close my eyes to sleep,
I will think of you
and my heart will remember to beat.

Writing in Blood

What unspoken thing is there left to write about,
when you already bleed from your heart,
making it the ink you write with.

With a fine tip like a needle that punctures
your veins to feed off your soft soul.

I write in the blood of my past that gave me
pain,
my present where I learn to heal from it,
and my future that might not be clear,
but is calling me in the distance.

There are things that still haunt me,
trying to weigh down my soul,
but with a pen as my weapon and blood as my
ammo,
I will conquer my demons that knock at my
door,
writing them on paper and exposing them for
who they are.

I write my life out on blank parchment,
not leaving any gory detail behind,

with my flesh attached
and my heart pulsating with every word
lining in perfect formation.

I have nothing to hide,
as my heart beats from the outside
and my demons are exposed,
leaving me vulnerable but true
with having nothing else to lose.

Cute

I saw you at first glance,
sending shivers through every inch of my body.

Killing me with your icy blue eyes,
sending a spark of warmth down my spine,
not knowing that it was going to turn into a
shard of ice,
piercing my heart, that once beat whole.

Now it beats in pieces shattered
around my broken soul,
still trying to flutter, like a newborn finch,
that's learning how to use their new wings
through a thunderstorm.

You came into my life almost just as fast as
I looked at you for the first time,
across the crowded room filled with strangers
but somehow all I saw was you.

You stole my heart quicker than I could take it
back,
but not nearly as fast as you destroyed my life,
with your southern charm and charismatic smile

that could fool anyone from miles away.

When we met you called me cute,
I was head over heels,
with my head in the clouds,
thinking that was the best compliment I could
receive.

Until I realized "cute" is what you call a puppy
or a baby,
or something that's so innocent and small
that hasn't experienced enough life yet.

It took me picking up the tiny pieces
scattered around on the floor,
like a jigsaw puzzle with a bunch of the
pieces missing to realize,
I am not cute.

I am built from sorrow and pain
that you will never know and maybe never cared
to,
but added to it instead.

I took that grief and anguish that created my
bloody wounds
and made them into scars that rest just
underneath the surface.

I am not cute.

I have scars that go deeper than the eyes can see
and a pretty face that is your first impression,
making me seem fragile,
like a porcelain doll sitting on the edge of a
shelf,
looking hollow inside.

But that doesn't make me "cute",
that makes me a warrior filled with beauty.

I am beautiful.

I'm a doll with a pretty face and a fragile outer
layer,
but what seems fragile is really made of stone,
from being dropped too many times
and learning how to harden my heart and make it
out of steel.

You may have left me with nothing but pain,
but led me on a path to finding my worth,
finding the beauty within me that has been
hiding all along.

My shattered heart,
that was once fluttering like a newborn flinch,
has now turned into a phoenix

rising from the ashes of the pain you caused
to make my heartbeat whole again.

Your icy blue eyes changed my life the first time
we met,
but not in the way you think.

They watered my "cute" isolated heart,
like a flower thirsty for the raindrops
that will make them bloom into something
beautiful,
something that turned them from a cute little
flower,
to blossomed petals filled with wonderment.

Maybe you weren't who I was looking for,
but I was able to find me through the sea of your
condescending ways,
and found the beauty that you overlooked in so
many ways.

She Told Me...

she's no teacher
and can't show me a single thing,
as she shows me how to crochet.

She told me she can't bake,
but makes me steaming hot peach cobbler
with ice cream on top.

She told me to sit up straight
and suck in my gut,
when she would slouch down herself.

She told me she never kept greeting cards or
hand drawn pictures,
because it's the thought that counts,
but that doesn't mean you hold on to it forever,
however, I found a cut out heart, tucked away in
her drawer neatly and tight.

She told me she'll never leave me,
but let's go of my hand in the end,
making me think all this time she's been lying to
me and telling a fib.

She told me she's proud of me
and I can do anything I want to do,
even when I think I'll amount to nothing.

She told me learning is the best adventure you'll
ever have
you just have to be open minded enough to take
the journey,
when I was too literal to see things clearly.

She told me reading will lead me to new worlds
and possibilities,
as long as you keep your glasses on and your
heart open,
when I hated the thought of touching a book
with one fingernail inching the cover.

She told me she would see the day I became
something great,
at this point I thought she was lying to me,
I thought all the things she's ever said were
things to just fool me.

She told me she would always be with me even
when I fall,
I know now as I'm writing this,
doing the things she said I would do,
I know she never lied to me at all, but I lied to
myself thinking no one would catch me.

She told me she would never leave my side,
now I know she never did, but she grew inside
me,
giving me the courage and strength, I needed to
become the person I am today.

She told me I could be anyone I wanted to be,
but only if I believed in what I was doing in my
heart's core.

I never thought writing would be the path I
chose,
but now I never believed in anything more.

She told me she's always cheering me on,
as much as I wish she was here to share this gift
I've found I possess,
I know she's with me, because I wouldn't have
been able to get this far without her.

She told me when I miss her,
just look up at the stars and she would be
looking at them too,
now that she's among them, I haven't gone a day
without looking up to the sky even when it's
bare and whisper, "Gramma, I did it."

And in my heart's core I know she's whispering
back, "I know."

Goodbye San Diego, Hello Me

I stood in the empty room,
with vacuum marks lining the bare carpet,
as a triangle pattern neatly draped from corner to
corner.

Staring at the indentures on the floor,
where furniture laid their legs,
marking where they once stood in this room.

I glanced out the window one last time,
watching the rain fall from the sky,
matching the tears trickling from my eyes.

Turning back to the empty space
a smile creeped up my face,
remembering the music
I would blare and dance the day away.

Before making my way to the door,
I pulled out my phone for one last dance,
in the place that made me feel safe.

In a place that made it okay
for me to cry my eyes out in grief,

for my heart to be vulnerable,
and also make me realize that my worth
costs a lot more than I gave myself credit for.

I laugh until my sides ache and
dance until my feet got sore
and knew it was time to go.

Walking towards the door
with a melancholy feeling
resting in the depth of my chest,
threatening to form a lump in my throat.

I strolled down the stairs taking my time
remembering what pictures used to hang on
these walls,
leaving their memories behind.

Departing through the front door,
leaving behind a house full of wonderful, sad,
exciting times,
filled with love and grief.

I drove out of a city I've made my own.

A city I didn't grow up in,
but grew in me.

It built me to be the person I am today.

I said goodbye to the fine sand that squished
between my toes,
the sun kissed highlights that graced my dark
autumn hair,
and early sunrises with late sunsets, that kissed
the city goodnight.

As I was packing up my things someone asked
me,
"Why would you want to leave your home, this
beautiful paradise?"

I gave a wistful smile and replied,
"I am not leaving my home. My home follows
me wherever I go, as long as I follow my heart,
my home will be waiting. This beautiful
paradise was a wonderful place that has sent me
on journeys and paths I never thought I would
explore. But now it has given me growth and
courage, to go find my next adventure. This was
a lovely home, but now it's time to find a new
one."

Driving through the city lights and ocean view, I
sighed to myself,
"Goodbye my sweet paradise. I will see you
again, but for now, I bid you farewell, spreading

the wings you gave me and fly to my new home,
with you in my heart forever."

I smile, knowing my adventures have just begun,
with windows down and the sun peeking
through the clouds,
I crossed the city border.

Goodbye San Diego,
Hello me.

Blanket Filled with Love

I pulled the cool crochet blanket up over my
chin,
just to the tip of my nose,
inhaling your scent of warm vanilla
the smell only you had that has

no other name for it, than just love.
It seeps off the silky yarn that held me tightly,
safe in its grasps,
like a hug that you would give me every night.

I remember watching you crochet,
being mesmerized by the yarn running through
your fingers creating something
so beautiful and amazing you'd share with me
one day.

A dark shadow creeped over my bed
as I pulled the blanket tightly around me,
looking at the patches you've sewed into the
worn yarn through all your hard work.

This is the third one you've made for me,
at the time I didn't know it would be the last,

but every time my heartaches
and I miss your hug I used to receive at night,

I held my blanket tight
almost feeling it squeezing me in return,
as vanilla from a fresh bean filled
my senses with a swirl of nothing but love.

I closed my eyes, pretending you're
still in the room across from me,
crocheting my next blanket filled with love
and adding a little mistake on purpose

Leaving your special signature behind,
keeping my heart full even when you're not
here.
Letting the darkness subside,
not scaring the little girl, you once knew so long
ago,

remembering a young woman has taken over
not needing to hide under the covers,
But using the blanket you made
filled with love as a shield,

fighting against the darkness that has tried to
swallow me up whole, after you left.
Holding the blanket close, inhaling
the fresh vanilla that still lingers,

maybe just a little less,
but still enough to fill my heart
as it sings a sweet melody
that puts me to sleep.

Story of Love

I want to write a love story,
but I don't know where to start,
with a wandering heart
and little to no experience.

I could write about you and me,
but was there really a you and me
or just a figment of what could be?

Staring at my spread-out notes
scattered throughout the lined paper,
trying to recount what it felt like
to be held in your arms so tightly.

Now left to the cold,
where my lips turn blue
and frostbite reaches my toes,
left alone to fend off the snow.

Maybe I wasn't meant to be in a love story,
with a heart so tender that
will bleed at the slightest touch
and will penetrate just at the thought of breaking
once more.

But with a fragile full heart and creative mind,
maybe I can take what we had,
whatever that might have been
and turn it into something that was extremely
beautiful
instead of something that ended tragically.

What we had, may not have lasted long
or ended the way either of us expected,
but if I close my eyes real tight,
I can still hear our laughs
and feel your lips on mine,
as they curl into a smile.

I want to write a love story,
so here it goes:

A girl with a wandering fragile soul meets
a boy with dangerously hypnotizing blue eyes
and a shell around his heart.

The girl broke the shell with one touch
of her breathtaking cold fingers
and he warms them in his soft strong working
hands.

He makes her fall in love with him
just long enough for him to re-build

his shell around his heart setting a curse
on anyone that loved him.

He pushed her away ashamed of
who he became,
but this only drew her closer
and made her want to show
him who he really was to her.

However, her fragile soul was too breakable
and started to shatter at the words he didn't
mean to say.

They both parted sadden at the outcome,
but one rainy day,
they were reunited and could see their mistakes.

They swore never to leave each other again
and lived happily ever after.

Only if this was a fairytale
and everything happened
the way we imagine it would.

Then maybe we could have endings this sweet
and hearts that don't break for eternity.

Forever 52

Today is your Birthday,
I hope wherever you are,
you help blow out the candles on the cake I
made you.

I don't remember how old you would have been,
because you said you were forever 52,
I believed that to be true
and told anyone that said otherwise, they were
wrong.

I thought you would be here forever
blowing out every candle for every year,
but now I know that the good die young
and the warriors go to heaven where the war is
never done.

Happy Birthday, to my angle from above still
fighting my battles with me
and even though a day doesn't go by without me
missing you,
I know you're with me every step of the way.

Never Left

You left without a goodbye,
leaving tears stinging my eyes.

Time flies without you by my side.

All that's left is memories fading away.

I wonder why it was your time as I start to cry
and say aloud,
"why did you disappear and leave me here, this
way?"

Tears fall from my cheek to the floor, as you
whisper in my ear,
"honey, I never went anywhere."

Then you played a sweet song
of a reminder through my mind.

I hear you humming along to a
song you once played on repeat.

I hear your laughter
through the humorous words I say.

I hear your guidance
in every step I take.

I see your smile in a
glimpse of the mirror.

I feel your worries and sadness
as tears leak from my eyes.

I feel your love and joy
through a hug and kiss.

I feel your touch grace
my cheek when I am blue.

I feel your love growing inside me,
making me a fighter, just like you.

Then you pat my cheek dry and say,
"you see? I never left and never will. We are
connected, a bond that will never stray. By your
side I will stay and forever in your heart, you'll
guide the way. I love you once and forever and
always."

Home

When I pass away,
there should be no sad face to see,
or tears for a lost soul.

I want to be remembered
and stories of joy to be shared
with everyone I may have met.

Dying should be a beautiful thing,
not a sad one.

I will be reunited with all the people that loved
me
and be with every person I love at once.

I will rejoice in my welcome home party
and still be with you every step you take.

So, when I pass, please don't be sad,
do not cry for a lost soul,
but if you must cry,

Cry with happiness that I completed
what I was meant to do here on earth,

cry because my soul is not lost but found.

And I will guide you until you join me in our
place,
we will call home.

Hourglass

Today I turn 23 and it feels bittersweet,
as I look in the mirror not feeling much older
than I did the year before,
but I see a slight crease where my lips and cheek
meet
from all the laughter and joy that makes my life
content and complete.

This year has flown by without a care,
no matter how tight I hold on to time that
trickles by.

Like the sand in an hourglass gliding grain by
grain
piling up on the other side of the vase,
not being able to hold on to the fine soft sand
falling out of my hands
even as I grasp with all my might.

The thing about time,
is that it doesn't care about the wrinkles under
your eyes
or the memories that fly by,

it only cares about one grain of sand trickling
down one at a time.

Life is fast and not a guarantee
to live on this sweet but bitter earth,
full of people that are kind as can be
and maybe hateful when they're first seen.

I don't know everything and never will,
but one thing I understand fully,
from my 23 years on this beautiful unfair world,
is that this life is short and we're all here for one
thing,
to live our lives to the fullest, ignoring our fears
and finding what makes us whole and feel like
time can standstill.

Life is like an hourglass,
filled with so much sand that moves slowly
and at the same time so fast you don't see it
streaming by
from one end to the other.

We never pay much mind to the sand
or how much of it is falling out of our hands,
because we get lost in it like a dessert that has no
end,
but the hard truth is, that the sand will eventually
stop

and we must take in every grain that falls down
as a gift.

Today I turn 23, looking back at the sand I've
collected
and hoping for more,
but not waiting to spare a moment
and live my life to the fullest with the sand I
already got.

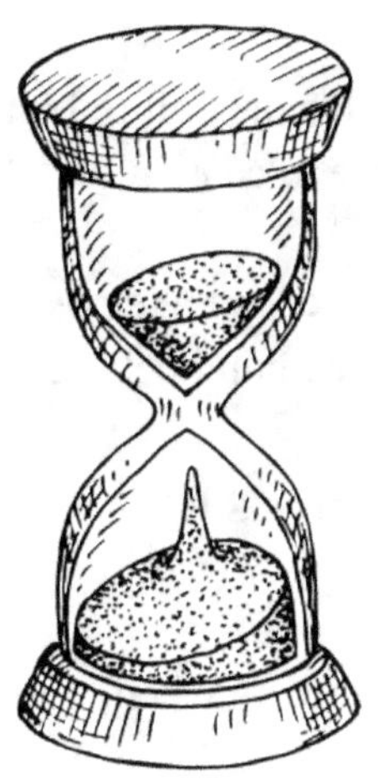

Mom

She carried me in her heart before
she could hold me in her arms.

She reached out for me before I knew
I needed someone to catch me.

She gave me all the love she possessed before
I even knew the meaning behind it.

She leant me her strength when I was at my
weakest.

She held back her tears when I needed her to be
strong.

She let me wipe my snot on her shirt
when I was in need of a tissue.

She hugged the breath out of me on my way to
school.

She never yelled at me through puberty
and kept chocolate on standby.

She knows all my sorrows and has seen all my
pain,
knowing my healing will take time but will
stand by my side.

She's seen me struggle and even though it was
hard,
let me grow into the person I came to be.

She was first my Mom, then my friend,
and forever my person, and to infinity.

She is my proctor, no matter how old I am,
guiding me through whatever life brings me
next.

She is my Mom.

What feels like yesterday…

this little human being could fit in the palm of
your hand,
so tiny and fragile,
not knowing what the world would bring her
way.

Now 23 very fast years later,
she's grown into a strong young woman,
with an unstoppable imagination ready for the
world to see.

She's seen sorrow,
she's known pain,
you've learned there's nothing to stop her
from taking on life's harsh lessons that come her
way.

Time has a funny way of melting through your
fingertips,
before you can grasp onto a moment,
as it turns into a memory.

What feels like yesterday,

you were reading to her from rhyming story
books
about multiple fishes of different colors
and a man that didn't like Green Eggs and Ham,
no matter where or anywhere he tried them.

Now she's writing storybooks of her own,
creating brand-new worlds
that comes from the depth of her mind,
finding ways to inspire others just by the words,
she writes down on blank paper.

What feels like yesterday,
you tucked her into bed,
kissing her on the head,
wishing the bad dreams to stay away,
so, she could close her eyes,
wondering about the future
she will one day hold in the palm of her hand.

You know you cannot give her the whole world
even though you try,
but you can embrace her for what may come,
making her fierce and brave,
ready to jump through any obstacle that gets in
her way.

She is ready for the world,
but it is not ready for her.

What feels like yesterday,
you were her hero that walked through
the door after an exhausting day,
where that hasn't changed.

Today she is the one walking through the door
greeting you
with a hug like she gave before,
but this time with a brand-new story
ready for you to explore.

Even though time has a harsh way of reminding
you
that your little princess is turning into a Queen,
you will always have memories that will never
leave you,
because she'll constantly remind you every day
of the little girl,
you read to so long ago
and stories that will follow her everywhere she
goes.

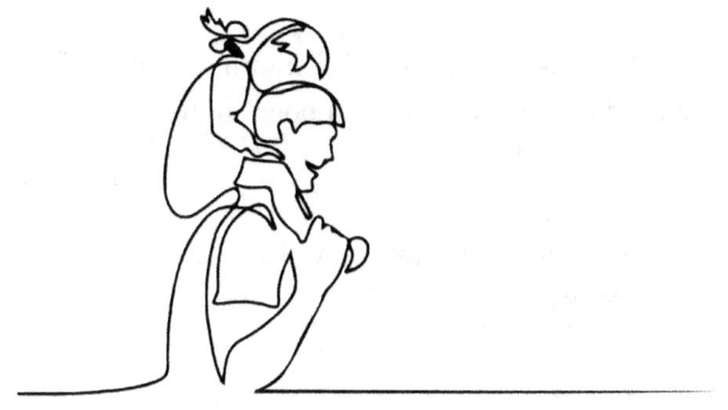

Forever and Always

He kisses her goodbye, as a tear rolls from her eye. He places his hand on her cheek and crests it away.

She pulls away and asks, "Why must you go?" He holds her tight as he whispers in her ear, "You know why."

"That's not a good enough reason," she would say in return.

He nods his head, "I know, but we both know I have to go."

He kisses her once more on the head and lets go as they pull away on the shore ahead.

He writes her everyday with a love filled letter, telling her he's counting the days until she's in his arms again.

He writes, "I love you forever and ever, always and infinity. As I write to you, please don't cry

even though you may shed a tear, know I'm in
your heart even when I'm not near."

She receives the letter, as tears flow through her
eyes dripping on his neatly written words,
Her heartaches with joy and sadness swirled into
one, as she sees him writing and thinking of the
right words to put down.

She knows he's in her heart and with her every
step she takes, but that doesn't take the pain of
missing him away.

She collects his letters and stores them in a box
where she still reads them every day, even when
he's right beside her as they turn old and gray.

She turns to look at him and asks, "Do you still
love me, like you did when you were away?"

He gives a perplexed look, "I never went
anywhere, I stayed right here." He pointed to her
heart as he smiles and finishes, "I love you
forever and ever, always and infinity."

She smiles and says, "I love you more."
He holds her tight, as they cherish the times they
don't have to spend apart.

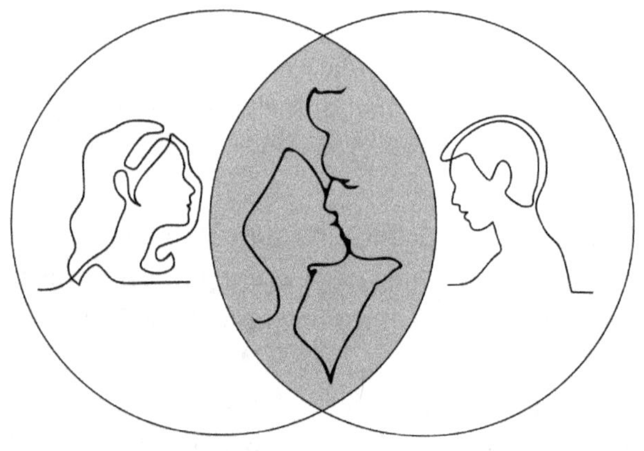

The Laugh

Her smile stretches from cheek to cheek,
as her laugh fills the air and becomes contagious
filling the people around her with joy.

The sun shines on her face,
as she waves her hand to say hi or bye,
but it doesn't matter which one
with happiness spreading on her face.

Her eyes are closed ever so lightly,
as to make a wish on a birthday candle,
wishing she could stay in this moment forever,
wishing she could freeze time and never leave
this sweet bliss.

I put her picture down and smile knowing she
got her wish.

One Day...

I'll meet you from across the way

One day you'll take my breath away
in a crowded place.

One day I'll introduce you to my family,
and they'll love you almost as much as I do,
because they'll look into my eyes
and know you're the one I've chosen to be my
always.

One day hopefully you'll ask them for my hand,
not because I need someone to make my
decisions for me,
but because it's respectful to the people who
raised me,
making me the independent woman I am today.

One day you'll realize how stubborn I can be,
but vulnerable when I want to be.

One day you'll know I'm always right,
but will listen to what you have to say,
even if I don't agree.

One day I'll wake up next to you
and stare into your eyes,
knowing there's nothing
more beautiful than love itself.

One day you'll hold me tight and never let go,
because you know if you let me slip through
your fingers,
it will be harder to regain your grasp.

One day your house will be mine
and we'll live across the street from my parents,
because you know they mean the world to me.

One day I'll wear a ring on my left hand
and never take it off, as I glance at it often,
reminding me you're always with me.

One day we're going to fight,
and I know we might not always see eye to eye,
but I know we can at least meet halfway.

One day I will meet you in a crowded place,
with a lost heart
and a missing piece to my jumbled jigsaw
puzzle.

One day you'll meet my eyes

and find me with your lost heart
and know you're not lost anymore.
64

One day seems so far away,
as I lie here alone,
but I know you'll be worth waiting for.

Famous

I don't want to be famous,
I don't care about the riches and glory,
that's not what I'm in it for.

I want my words to be
hanging on someone's wall
and for them to be able to quote it by heart.

I want my words to act like lyrics,
as they sing off someone's tongue,
smooth and slow.

I want my words to be arrows of wisdom
that aim straight for your soul
and make you want more.

I want my words to bring a tear to the
corner of your eye,
because you know you're not alone in this unfair
world.

I want my words to latch on to someone's soul
and never let go,
making a difference in their lives,

they never knew they yearned for.

I don't want to be famous;
I just want to be heard.

About Author

KC Hampton is pursuing her BFA in creative writing at Full Sail University. She is aspiring to become a novelist, specializing in Realistic Drama, Comedy/Drama, Horror, and Tragedy. Her flash fiction pieces have been published in *Adelaide Literary Magazine No.52*, *CaféLit Magazine*, and in *Rose City Sisters*. She is a member of AWP and has taken classes in film and creative writing. KC is not only a full-time writer, but also a single mom to an adorable Coton de Tulear puppy. Born a traveler and currently growing her career in Orlando Florida.

www.ingramcontent.com/pod-product-compliance
Lightning Source LLC
Chambersburg PA
CBHW071946120726
48001CB00005B/2057